by

DAVID LANDAU

Music & Lyrics by

NIKKI STERN

SAMUEL FRENCH, INC.

45 West 25th Street NEW YORK 10010
7623 Sunset Boulevard HOLLYWOOD 90046
LONDON TORONTO

ISBN 0 573 62664 2

Printed in the U.S.A.

IMPORTANT BILLING AND CREDIT REQUIREMENTS

All producers of MURDER AT CAFÉ NOIR *must* give credit to the Author of the Play in all programs distributed in connection with performances of the Play and in all instances in which the title of the Play appears for purposes of advertising, publicizing or otherwise exploiting the Play and/or a production. The name of the Author *must* also appear on a separate line, on which no other name appears, immediately following the title, and *must* appear in size of type not less than fifty percent the size of the title type.

INTRODUCTION

The interactive mystery play was first invented over ten years ago as an attempt to mix environmental theater with audience involvement. The goal was to allow the audience to experience the drama as if they were extras in a movie. The entire production, from script to props, direction to location, was oriented towards encompassing the audience in the world of the mystery and not, as has become the norm today, merely with the game of solving the mystery. The latter was, and should always be, a secondary entertainment. It is the story of the characters which must always take center stage—a story of desperate people in desperate situations that are compelled to perform desperate acts. This does not mean that the show is void of comedy, but rather that the humor comes from the characters and not at their expense.

In a true mystery there can only be one logical killer, pointed out not only by the clues, but by the motivation, personality and situation the character finds himself/herself in. While there are a number of other likely suspects, this character is the inevitable culprit. The mystery has been sown well when the average of correct guesses is 10%. By the end of the play, when all is revealed, the audience should sigh with a resounding "Of course, I should have thought of that!"

The interactive mystery play offers theater patrons, performers and producers many unique opportunities. The audience can be taken to the very edge of suspense and then suddenly dropped into a humorous release of tension. The characters can become so real that they can reach out and touch the audience, literally. The theatrical fourth wall is placed *behind* the audience. If done correctly, the interactive play can be the most involving form of theater possible.

David Landau
September 16, 1993
Creator of the first interactive mystery play, Dec. 1982
Member of The Dramatists Guild and Mystery Writers of America.

NOTES ON PRODUCTION

PERFORMANCE SPACE. The following play has been designed to be performed in a dining room, dinner theater, night club, theater-in-the-round or a thrust stage where the acting area is level with the first row. The intention is to make the audience feel like they are actually in the location of the story. The performance is a sort of reverse theater in the round, with action performed around the circumference of the seating area, as well as down the aisles and in the center. The audience should be seated at tables, either cocktail style or dining tables. Tables could be added in front of the first rows in the case of thrust or arena stages with bleacher seating. Audience members can even be seated on stage.

SCENES & BREAKS. The script is formatted into five 15 minute scenes. Between each scene is time to serve a course of a meal, serve drinks, or play dance music as desired. During these breaks the characters mingle and reveal information to the audience in a one on one manner. The script can easily be adapted to eliminate some of these breaks. If this is the desire, black-outs should take place between scenes with the intermission scheduled after scene 3. There should also be a musical break between scenes 4 & 5 that will allow audience members to hand in their guesses as to "whodunit."

MUSICAL NUMBERS. The musical numbers in this play have been designed to be performed to a music tape provided with the licensing of the script. Lead sheets are also provided for the actors. Some producers have hired piano players in the past, but this is not necessary and often contrary to the intent of the "surprise" musical interlude.

AWARDING PRIZES. The "Sleuth Sheets" are collected by the characters between scenes 4 & 5 and handed to the stage manager for sorting. Scene 5 is performed after all the guesses have been collected. After the curtain call, the correct answers are handed to the main character, who reads out the names of the successful sleuths. Generally, all correct answers are placed in a hat and a character draws one name. A prize is then awarded to the patron by a cast member.

CAST

RICK ARCHER — A private eye who's always wanted to be Bogart or Mitchum in one of those 40s film noir movies, and has not gotten his chance.

MADAM TOUREAU — A lady who's seen it all while managing the Café Noir—where everything is for sale.

SHEILA WONDERLY — Her real name is Sheilda Schickelmeier. Once a spoiled rich girl, she took a job at Café Noir and learned about life the hardest way of all, becoming hardened in the process.

ANTHONY CAIRO — A dealer in the black market working Café Noir to avoid the St. Vincent police. He has two scars, one on either side of his face.

MARIE LARUE — The Creole illegitimate daughter of a Voodoo priestess and a St. Vincent's political figure. She sells spells and fortunes at Café Noir.

SIMON GUTTERMAN — A British barrister who lost his standing when he became implicated in a scandal of having affairs with wealthy female clients. He now caters to the clientele of Café Noir. Simon is always looking for a quick way to make it to the top.

THURSBY — A two bit gun runner.
VANGILDER — A Dutch blackmailer.
RIGFIELD — A British cop from St. Vincent.
(All three are played by the same actor.)

NOTE: ALL CHARACTERS DRESS IN BLACK & WHITE ONLY

The room is decorated to look tropical, but everything is in black and white and shades of gray. A sign hangs on one wall proclaiming "Café Noir". An old radio stands by a small bar. During cocktails the sound of the waves breaking on the beach and the sound of gulls are heard. Tables should have six to eight place settings, forcing strangers to sit with one another. Black or gray table cloths and gray or black candles should be on each table. Patrons will get their own drinks from the bar.

PRE-SHOW

As patrons enter, they are shown to their table by MADAM TOUREAU. On every table is a Sleuth Sheet asking who-dunit and why and a copy of a newspaper front page, which patrons will no doubt take turns reading. It reads as follows:

• •

THE GRENADINE ISLETS INQUIRER
BODY OF ANDRE GAUVREAU DISCOVERED BY TOURISTS

Early this morning the cold blue corpse of Andre Gauvreau was spotted washed ashore on the north beach of Tobago Cay by twenty tourists with cameras on a boat tour from St. Vincent. Clad in a white Giorgio Armani suit with a bold pink Sergio Valente tie, the body of Mr. Gauvreau was originally mistaken by the tourists for the great albino turtle. After beating off three hungry albatrosses, Kingston authorities retrieved the corpse and determined Mr. Gauvreau had died from two gun shot wounds. Andre Gauvreau, owner of the Islet Shipping Co., Grenadine Import/Exports and the Café Noir on Mustique, was a very powerful and often feared figure in the area, rumored to have been involved with smuggling, the black market and prostitution. He leaves behind no immediate family, though six women have filed claims against his estate for child support. The Café Noir will remain open tonight, drinks are half price.

RESORTS INTERNATIONAL TO OPEN CASINO

The first casino in the Grenadines will open on Tobago Cay next—

• •

ANTHONY CAIRO will enter, looking and acting the same as the patrons. His nervousness could be mistaken for shyness as he scans the faces of the people present and subtly moves about during the seating period, carrying a stuffed, sealed envelope. He places down an envelope at a small table with a radio on it. MARIA LARUE enters as if just another patron. She sees Cairo and smiles. Cairo leaves the envelope and walks away, nursing a drink. Maria walks to the table and exchanges a small wrapped bundle for Cairo's envelope, then disappears into the kitchen. Cairo walks back, takes the bundle and heads for the front door when SIMON GUTTERMAN enters. Cairo quickly changes his direction and heads for the kitchen. On the way he stops and puts his glass down on a table—where he leaves the bundle as well. (Inside the bundle is a voodoo doll made of white cloth with two needles through the heart.) The sounds of the waves and gulls fades and the lights dim.

CAFÉ NOIR

Scene 1

(Music begins to play. A match is lit and a spotlight comes up on RICK ARCHER as he lights his own cigarette. He is dressed as a typical P.I. character.)

RICK. Have you ever wished you could just close your eyes and wake up in the past, at a point in your life that seemed a trivial decision, but turned out to be the most important and perhaps the worst mistake you ever made? Sure you have. I have lots of times. But this time it was different. This time I wished I had made a different choice, but deep down I knew that I wouldn't—that I couldn't.

Right now you're probably asking yourself, what the hell is this guy talking about? Well, I'll tell you, in all the sordid details. First we'll start with who I am. That will come in handy later. My handle is Richard Archer, but everyone calls me Just Plain Rick. I was weaned on TV reruns of Bogart and Mitchum movies and after graduating last in my class at the John Jay College of Criminology I became a private dick. You know, the sleazy guys that disgruntled spouses hire to follow their better halves. *(Music starts under.)* The snoops that cheap insurance companies hire to get snapshots of claimants playing athletic sports; the fools who think life could really be like those romantic movies of the forties.

RICK. *(Cont.)* Well, this time it was. Even the way it all started, with some tacky dressed, well-to-do drunk hiring me in a bar in Reno to find his runaway daughter. He paid me five thousand clams in advance and plied me with a picture of a dame that had more curves than the west coast highway. Daddy's little girl had been nursing a degree in Grenada when the troops took the beach away from the sun worshipers, and after hearing about her from almost every American soldier on the island, I traced the doll to a few tiny forgotten islets in the eastern Caribbean called the Grenadines. And that's what brought me here, to Café Noir.

(The lights come up over the entire audience. RICK sings "Café Noir" as he walks through the crowd.)

RICK.
HUSTLERS ON HIATUS
TOUGH GUYS OFF THE TAKE
DAMES WHO PAY FOREVER
FOR AN INNOCENT MISTAKE
BEEN ABROAD SO LONG
NOW IT'S THE ONLY LIFE THEY KNOW
DENIZEN OR DROP-OUT
THEY'VE GOT NOWHERE ELSE TO GO

AT CAFÉ NOIR,
A CHEAP ISLAND BAR
THE LONELINESS HANGS LIKE A CLOUD
MOST OF YOU
WILL BE PASSING ON THROUGH
AND THE REST WILL GET LOST IN THE CROWD
YOU'VE COME TO CAFÉ NOIR
AN ALL PURPOSE BAR
BUT DON'T LOOK FOR THE WELCOMING CREW
IF YOUR MONEY'S OKAY
THEN YOU MIGHT AS WELL STAY
THOUGH I WOULDN'T IF I WERE YOU

(Music under.)

RICK. (Cont.) It was the sleaziest club around, but then again it was the only one and the characters that hung out there were a frightening sight. *(He grimaces at the audience.)* The manager was a Madam Toureau—a lady who'd seen more of the underside of life than the motion picture rating system.

MADAM.
EVERY NOW AND THEN
A FANCY SHIP MAY COME TO CALL
THEN THE PLACE GETS OF LIVELY
WHAT WITH PASSENGERS AND ALL
EASY TO BELIEVE IN LUCK
NO MATTER WHAT THE COST
TIL THE SHIP SETS SAIL
AND THEN IT'S EASY TO FEEL LOST

	CHORUS.
AT CAFÉ NOIR	HERE ON THE
A CHEAP ISLAND BAR	ISLAND
DRINKING CARIBBEAN	
BOOZE	YOU LOSE
TRYIN' TO GET STIFF	STUCK ON THE
WHILE YOU'RE WONDER-	
ING IF	ISLAND
YOU'VE GOT ANYTHING	
ELSE YOU CAN LOSE	YOU CHOSE
CAFÉ NOIR	OUT ON THE
YOUR TYPICAL BAR	ISLAND
DESIGNED TO HELP	
PATRONS FORGET	OOH

NO THE LIQUOR'S NOT SMOOTH
BUT IT MIGHT HELP TO SOOTHE
ANY LINGERING TRACE OF REGRET

(Music under, and continues.)

RICK. Here, every face had a past. Every nerve strung so tight, it was like a string orchestra, perched at that moment before the conductor's baton swung down and started that last movement. It was here that I found my runaway.

(SHEILA enters from the front door. She looks nervous.)

MADAM. Sheila, you're late!
SHEILA. I was detained.
MADAM. Detained?
SHEILA. By the St. Vincent police, Madam Toureau. They've been asking me questions for hours.
MADAM. Actually, I'm surprised you came in at all. I thought you might be in mourning.
SHEILA. And I thought you might be.
MADAM. Well then, we're both wrong, n'est ce pas? Our customers await.
SHEILA. *(Looking at audience.)* Let them wait.
MADAM. You were in such a rush to leave with André last night, you didn't even notice you dropped one of your earrings.

(MADAM holds up one earring and then tosses it at her. SHEILA catches it and sings.)

SHEILA.
ANSWERING TO NO ONE
MAKING MY OWN RULES
FREE TO CUT MY LOSSES
AND TO WALK AWAY FROM FOOLS
HEY, I MAY SOUND CYNICAL
BUT HEY, THAT'S HOW I SOUND
THE ISLAND'S NOT A HALF-BAD SPOT
AND THIS IS WHAT I'VE FOUND

	CHORUS.
AT CAFÉ NOIR	LIFE ON THE
IT'S A CHEAP ISLAND BAR	ISLAND
NO ONE CARES WHAT YOU'VE DONE	
OR WHO YOU ARE	SO FAR
YOU CAN COME, YOU CAN GO	
AND THERE'S ALWAYS THE SHOW	
THAT PLAYS OUT EVERY NIGHT AT THE BAR	CAFÉ
YOU CAN DISAPPEAR	NOIR
YOU CAN CRY IN YOUR BEER	
IT'S WHATEVER YOU WANT IT TO BE	
YEAH, WE TAKE UP SPACE	
BUT IN THIS KIND OF PLACE	
THERE'S AN ODD SENSE OF BEING FREE	WE'RE FREE

ALL.
THAT'S WHY CAFÉ NOIR
IS THE PERFECT HOME FOR ME

(SHEILA looks at her earring, then clutches it in thought. She notices RICK staring at her. He winks. She turns and starts to walk to the back door. RICK turns to the audience.)

RICK. Sheila Wonderly. At least that's the name she was going by when I found her. Her real name was Sheilda Schickelmeier. I can't say I blamed her for changing it, but I got the feeling it wasn't just her name that had done a lot of changing since Daddy saw her last. Getting her to come back home to Burning Rock Arkansas wasn't going to be an easy task, especially with the suspicious death of the club's owner—a man who went through women like Congress goes through tax relief, taking away all that's good and leaving behind a stripped framework of sorrow and broken promises. Even if my runaway was ready to run home, the cops wouldn't have let her. To earn the rest of my clams I had to get close to her and get her out of the mess she was in deeper than even she knew. *(RICK changes his demeanor and turns to MADAM.)* Madam Toureau?

MADAM. Politer people call me that. You're fresh blood around her. What can I do you for?

RICK. A day of work. I'm an American fellow down on his luck. I just need a few more greenbacks to buy myself a ticket out of here.

MADAM. And what makes you think I could use a stranger in my place?

RICK. I read the owner passed away with the outgoing tide and figured there'd be a few faces that might decide they didn't have to show tonight.

MADAM. You're a smart guy. *(She checks her watch.)* Maybe there are a few defaults this evening. Maybe I could use an extra hand. What makes you worth the risk?

RICK. No risk. At the end of the night, you can pay me what you think I've been worth.

MADAM. Sounds fair, and foolhardy. What are you running from?

RICK. I'm not running from anything.

MADAM. A lot of people say that. They're just trying to fool themselves. We all have our little something to hide and protect. Something we don't want anyone else to get too close to. *(She turns to a patron.)* You know what I'm talking about, don't you?

(If the person says "Yes", Madam answers "Of course you do, we already know all about you." If they say "No", she gives a small laugh and replies, "Oh, but I know you do.")

MADAM. *(Cont. To RICK.)* Let me explain something to you, Mr.—ah—

RICK. Rick. Just plain Rick.

MADAM. Alright, Mr. just plain Rick. This is the Café Noir. It may look like a dump at times but it's a very important place in these parts. It's a middle ground where the dishonest can be honest about it. Where everyone is entitled to their secrets and everyone else is entitled to find them out. It's a place where anything and everything is for sale, and there's always a buyer. It's the only place like it in the world, Rick, because the shadows here offer total acceptance, no matter who you are or what you've done. Take our friend over here.

(MADAM walks up to a young woman patron.)

MADAM. *(Cont.)* Once the debutante of the decade, until it was discovered she had been running a prostitution ring out her dormitory room at Radcliffe. You should have never given discounts to the professors, dear. It may have improved your transcripts but *(MADAM motions to her escort.)* look at where it got you. And another loyal patron—

(MADAM walks to a man patron.)

MADAM. *(Cont.)* He collected on nineteen life insurance policies, in nineteen different states in just four months—drowning deaths each time. Too bad the insurance company went bankrupt before you could finish collecting. If ever you try it again, sweetheart, try nineteen different insurance companies. And here's another regular—

(MADAM walks to another woman.)

MADAM. *(Cont.)* Such an innocent face. Who would have thought that as a teenager she carved up her stepparents with a Remco electric knife on the night before Thanksgiving and served them to their relatives the next day? You would have gotten away with it too, if your stepfather's gold tooth hadn't somehow gotten mixed in with the stuffing. *(Back to RICK.)*

You see, Rick, everyone has secrets, until they come to Café Noir.

RICK. *(To the last woman picked out.)* Remind me never to come to your place for dinner.

MADAM. She's the chef at the Grenadine Hyatt. But we were talking about you, Mr. Rick.

RICK. I wasn't.

MADAM. What are you running away from?

RICK. I'll tell you a secret, Madam Toureau. I never run away, from anything. That's my problem.

MADAM. Could be a very dangerous one around here. You're hired, Rick—for tonight. I like to live dangerously—lets you know you're still alive. You can start by taking drink orders and we'll have to get you a white jacket.

(MADAM starts for the kitchen, but GUTTERMAN intercepts her.)

GUTTERMAN. Do you think that wise, Madam? Especially with the St. Vincent police looking so closely into—

MADAM. I'm still the manager here.

GUTTERMAN. Perhaps you've managed more than just André's cafe.

MADAM. You amuse me, Gutterman.

(MADAM exits to kitchen. GUTTERMAN looks suspiciously at RICK and then goes after her. RICK turns to the closest table.)

RICK. Would anyone here care for a drink?

MARIA. *(To RICK.)* Is it true what I heard you say?

RICK. Depends on what you heard me say.

MARIA. *(She walks to him.)* That you never run away, from anything?

RICK. Yeah. I seem to have a problem with that. I'm like that stupid Scottish terrier we had when I was growing up.

One day it decided to chase the neighbor's car. Unfortunately, that day the neighbors were moving to Alaska.

MARIA. I love a man with conviction.

SHEILA. *(Stepping forward.)* Most of the men around here have been convicted several times. I guess that explains why you've made love to so many of them.

MARIA. At least I don't go for the highest bidders. I just love to love—not to make money.

(SHEILA tries to slap MARIA, but RICK catches her hand before it lands on MARIA's cheek. SHEILA pulls her hand away from him, angry. THURSBY suddenly enters through the front door. He is dressed in a black leather jacket.)

THURSBY. Maria, baby—I think we've hit pay dirt.

(THURSBY gives RICK a cold stare and starts to approach.)

THURSBY. Who are you?

SHEILA. Someone new your girlfriend's taken a liking to, Thursby. *(To RICK.)* Oh, this is Thursby—he's a three time offender wanted in Jamaica, Barbados, and the Bahamas for gun smuggling, manslaughter and being a public nuisance. Thursby, meet Rick. He's a total stranger that the Madam just put on for the night and your Voodoo queen has got the evil eye for. *(Back to RICK.)* Perhaps I should leave the three of you alone.

(THURSBY pulls out a switch blade. As SHEILA starts to walk away, RICK grabs her hand and twirls her into his arms.)

RICK. Going? Without a good-bye kiss?

(RICK swoops her into a heavy kiss. MARIA looks angry. THURSBY looks confused. As the kiss lingers on, MARIA storms off to the kitchen. THURSBY, perplexed, closes his knife and goes after her.)

THURSBY. Maria? Maria, I found something that's gonna make us rich.

(Once they're gone, RICK ends the kiss, bringing SHEILA back up for air. She immediately slaps him.)

RICK. Well, you got me into it. I figured the least you could do was get me out of it.

SHEILA. Smart guy, huh? Well, smart guys aren't my type.

(SHEILA exits to the kitchen. CAIRO, still observing from the corner applauds.)

CAIRO. Very good, Mr. Rick. Yes—it's always nice to meet a man who knows how to handle a truly volatile situation. Perhaps your talents in that area might extend beyond just domestic troubles?

RICK. Perhaps. Mr—?

CAIRO. Cairo, Anthony Cairo. A dealer in the black market. I can get you anything, for a price.

RICK. What is it you can't seem to get for yourself?

CAIRO. Insightful as well? You're a man of many surprises, Mr. Rick—yes! Freedom, to answer your question. Freedom to leave this time forgotten islet. Have you noticed that everything and everyone here seems to have set foot out of a 1940s movie? Have you ever been to a tropical island where everything was so—gray? And just look, look at the name of this club—Café Noir.

RICK. Then you fit right in here. Why would you want to leave?

CAIRO. I have more than enough reasons, Mr. Rick, let me assure you. Wouldn't my wanting to leave fit right in as well?

RICK. With the murder of the club's owner, your wanting to leave may fit in all too well. What I don't get is what's stopping you.

CAIRO. *(A slight laugh.)* Gauvreau's death. He was to supply me with not only the passport, but the passage upon one of his ships. You see, Mr. Rick—

RICK. Just plain Rick.

CAIRO. Yes, yes—Mr. just plain Rick. I am a man without an identity. A citizen of no country. A fugitive with a new face—courtesy of the talents of a doctor friend of M. Gauvreau, whom I've had to pay dearly. *(He turns to a patron.)* I just wish you had used some anesthesia.

RICK. A little trouble with the law?

CAIRO. If only it were that simple. I once had the folly to redirect a certain shipment of black market goods in order to affect a higher personal profit. Shall we say the supplier of these goods did not appreciate my entrepreneurial instincts. A change of facial scenery became a necessity for life. My new passport and the ticket are in a gray envelope in M. Gauvreau's office. As an associate of M. Gauvreau's I am being watched closely by the St. Vincent police. But you are a stranger, a face they would easily forget if they noticed at all.

RICK. Thanks a lot, fellah.

CAIRO. I am prepared to make this small gesture worth your while.

(CAIRO pulls a few bills of foreign currency and pushes them into RICK's pocket.)

RICK. Breaking into a deceased man's office doesn't sound like that small of a gesture to me.

(RICK pulls the bills out of his pocket. CAIRO pulls a key on a gray ribbon out of his pocket and dangles it.)

CAIRO. Even if one were to have a key?

RICK. I suppose that might make it a little easier, but—

CAIRO. The office in question happens to be behind the kitchen.

RICK. Then why don't you just do it yourself?

CAIRO. The walls have eyes, my friend. Yes—the walls have eyes.

(CAIRO drops the key into RICK's hand, on top of the bills, and leaves for the kitchen. He stops as he passes the bar. In the shadows behind it lurks GUTTERMAN. CAIRO exits quickly. GUTTERMAN laughs to himself and raises a drink in toast to RICK. RICK turns his back to GUTTERMAN and looks at the key, then pockets everything.)

RICK. *(To audience.)* Okay folks. What would you have done? This is the audience participation portion of the show. By a show of hands you will determine what I do next. How many think I should sneak into the deceased's office for Mr. Cairo's gray envelope? *(There will be a show of hands.)* And how many for ignoring Mr. Cairo and just pursuing the dame with a set of parabolas that would send a construction crew into double overtime—Sheila Wonderly that is.

(Another show of hands. RICK will do whatever the majority rules, with the appropriate response.)
*(**VERSION A**—If they vote for him to get the envelope:)*

RICK. Sending me into the back room. Not a very safe way to play things, but who wants to live long when life's a bore. Thanks a lot. Okay, majority rules—but if I don't come back in the same condition, it'll be on your heads.

*(**VERSION B**—If they vote for him not to go for the envelope:)*

RICK. Not a very curious crowd, are we? I know where your minds are at. You want me to tail Ms. Wonderly's tail. Okay, majority rules—not that I mind. Maybe there'll be a few fringe benefits I'll owe you some thanks for later.

(BOTH versions continue here.)

MADAM. *(Entering.)* Ladies and Gentleman, and I use the term indiscriminately—this evening's next course is a little specialty from the kitchen of the Grenadine Hyatt.

(EVERYONE enters. During the serving, characters will interact with the patrons.)

CAIRO asks various people at different tables if they have seen the small bundle he misplaced earlier. If asked, he says it contained a present he bought for his mother. He will also ask people if they might want to buy anything on the black market—caviar, Russian vodka, electronic goods? As he asks, Cairo pulls from one pocket a small jar of caviar, a small bottle of vodka from the other pocket and then opens his coat to reveal an electronics catalogue. CAIRO will reveal that the police questioned THURSBY about the murder. If questioned, he will admit to being questioned himself. "Why pay legal prices? Whatever you want, I can get it for you. Duty free. The market is always in the black when you deal with Cairo Imports.

GUTTERMAN asks people if they know what it was RICK and CAIRO were discussing. He will ask patrons if they need legal counsel, his specialty being criminal defense. He will also flirt with the ladies, suggesting a romantic rendezvous later this evening. He will reveal that the police questioned MARIA about the murder. If asked, he will admit to being questioned himself. "Legal counsel for questionable legal activities, criminal defense and untraceable tax free investments my specialty. It's such a lovely island, certainly we can't have dirty money spoiling the view."

MARIA asks people if they know anything about the stranger Rick. She offers to sell people spells of attraction, success, to ward off the evil eye and just about anything else. She reveals that the police questioned CAIRO about the murder. If asked, she'll admit the police questioned her as well. "Candles, potions, incense and spells for all purposes and occasions. 24 hour service, just dial 1-800-Voodoo. House calls available, birthday parties my specialty."

THURSBY asks people whether RICK came on to his girl MARIA, or if she came on to him. He also tries to get people interested in buying weapons. He pulls a high tech weapons catalogue from his jacket and points out what he can get wholesale. He reveals the police questioned Gutterman about the murder. If asked, he will admit they questioned him as well. "Don't get mad—*(Opens his coat to reveal guns of various sizes and grenades.)*—Get even. The latest in high tech extermination tools—new and used. Remember your trip always with a grenade from the Grenadines. Got a special on scud missiles and anti-personnel devices."

MADAM asks people if they are enjoying their visit to the Grenadines. She warns them about the sand-flies on the beach and that the sharks come in around sunset every night this time of year. If there's anything they wish to know about the islets, they can ask her. She reveals the police questioned Maria about the murder. If asked, she'll admit she was questioned as well.

SHEILA flirts with the men and suggests that she could show them a good time for the right price. She insists her men have a gold card, though she only accepts cash. She reveals that the police questioned MADAM TOUREAU about the murder. If asked, she'll admit she was questioned as well. RICK will follow her to the table and try to get her to talk with him, but she will ignore him and walk away. "Special discount for gold and corporate card members. Wonder-lay—the name says it all."

RICK will ask people if they've learned anything about the other characters. He will catch up to SHEILA at her table after she's been there a while and is about to leave. He tries to tell her that her daddy hired him to find her and bring her home, but she keeps walking away, ignoring him. If the vote was for him to get the envelope, he will eventually disappear into the kitchen and come out again later and wink at the crowd. If the vote was the other way, he'll just follow SHEILA, trying to get her to listen to him.

Scene 2

(Music intro. Lights up. Depending on which version was voted on earlier, RICK either displays a grey envelope to the audience or is following SHEILA as she exits.)

*(**VERSION A**—To get envelope. RICK shows the audience he has the Grey envelope then pockets it. Skip to bottom of next page.)*
*(**VERSION B**—To tail SHEILA. RICK catches her alone before she can exit.)*

RICK. Actually, I'm not surprised to find you in a place like this.

SHEILA. Where would you be surprised to find me?

RICK. A convent for one, but certainly not in a dead man's café.

SHEILA. Some men, even when they're dead, can control a woman.

RICK. And you like it that way.

SHEILA. Why would I?

RICK. Because then you can blame whatever trouble you're in on someone else, someone who isn't around to say otherwise.

SHEILA. *(Leaning in, her lips almost touching his.)* You're such a smart guy, aren't you, mister Rick? Always knowing what to say—how to say it—who to say it to. What do you want, a medal?

RICK. I can think of something I'd like a whole lot more. Something a lot softer—wetter—sweeter.

(SHEILA licks RICK's lips.)

SHEILA. Something like that?
RICK. Something like that? And something like this.

(RICK kisses SHEILA. She bites his lip. He yells and steps back.)

RICK. But not that.
SHEILA. I thought you were a tough guy.

(SHEILA starts to leave.)

RICK. You think all guys are tough guys so you can be heartless towards them before they can be heartless towards you.
SHEILA. What do you know?
RICK. I know you're running away but never getting anywhere. Because what you're really running away from is always right behind you, like your shadow, only deeper.
SHEILA. Don't pretend to know me, Mr. Just Plain Rick.

(SHEILA turns to leave again.)

RICK. I never pretend.

(SHEILA exits. RICK rubs his lip.)
*(**BOTH** versions continue here.)*

(MARIA comes up behind RICK and startles him with the next line.)

MARIA. I hear you came to take little miss love-for-sale back to Daddy.

RICK. Where'd you hear that? *(Glaring at audience member.)* Did you tell her that?

MARIA. Forget about her. She's bad karma. She left with André last night—part of their deal was he got her once a week. The rest of the week he got her the biggest spenders in the Caribbean. She won't be going any further away than St. Vincent Prison.

RICK. What if she didn't do it?

MARIA. A lot of people in St. Vincent Prison didn't do it—or at least not with the right people.

RICK. You sound like you know what you're talking about, Maria.

MARIA. I should. My mother died in that prison and for no other crime than that she loved the wrong man.

RICK. Your father?

MARIA. He was a politician—white bread and British to the hilt. Then one day on a tour of the outer islets he saw my mother and was possessed by her magic. Odd match—he an Oxford appointee of the Queen, she a voodoo priestess and descendant of a runaway slave. It was a time of political upheaval. Both the French and the African factions wanted more voice in the government. But the rich British minority feared a loss of control. For the love of her people, my mother became their voice and my father began to lose favor. After a bombing of a police station my mother was arrested, even though she had been in the arms of my father at the time. My father was transferred by the British parliament to the Falkland Islands. I was born in St. Vincent Prison, the same cell my mother died in. Soon after it was discovered the bombing was the work of the radical Liberté French party.

(MARIA is on the verge of tears.)

RICK. I'm sorry Maria. Nothing can make up for the raw deal life hands some of us. Your father?

MARIA. He doesn't even know I exist.

(MARIA folds into his arms in tears and just then THURSBY enters. He pulls out his knife.)

THURSBY. Let go of her.

(MARIA turns as THURSBY approaches menacingly.)

RICK. *(Raising his hands.)* You got things a little wrong, fellah.
THURSBY. Yeah, sure. Like I got it wrong with that frog André.
MARIA. *(Meaning shut up.)* THURSBY!
RICK. *(Beginning to back up.)* You mean André Gauvreau?
THURSBY. He was always groping after her as if he didn't have enough already.

(THURSBY takes a jab at RICK, who jumps back.)

MARIA. Thursby! No—
THURSBY. Now you come in here, nosing around.

(THURSBY takes another jab at RICK, who avoids him. THURSBY continues to back RICK at knife point around the room.)

RICK. Thursby, didn't your mother ever tell you not to play with sharp things?
MARIA. Thursby, please—*(to RICK.)* He's insanely jealous. He doesn't know what he's saying.
RICK. It's not what he's saying that's got me worried.

(THURSBY takes another jab at RICK, who jumps back. By now RICK is standing near the table with the radio, where there is a glass of liquid. RICK grabs the glass and throws it in THURSBY's face. THURSBY staggers back, raising his arms in shock. RICK grabs the hand with the knife and pulls it down, twisting THURSBY's arm around his back. MADAM enters.)

MADAM. What's going on here?

RICK. Thursby was just showing me some of the dance steps he learned from West Side Story.

(RICK pulls the knife away from THURSBY and shows it to MADAM.)

MADAM. I see—You just met his girl named Maria.

(RICK releases THURSBY, who rubs his hand and then storms off. MARIA goes after him.)

RICK. *(To audience member who got wet from the thrown drink.)* Sorry about getting you wet like that. But I had a choice, you get wet or I get stabbed. It wasn't a tough choice.

MADAM. Well, you really do liven a place up, just plain Rick.

(MADAM takes knife from RICK.)

RICK. Tell me about André, Madam. I'm sure you know more about him than anyone else, even the police.

MADAM. Are you the police?

RICK. No Madam. I'm my own man—*(To woman in audience.)* which is the loneliest kind of all.

MADAM. Then why should I tell you anything?

RICK. Because the longer André's murderer is loose, the longer the St. Vincent police have to dig deep into this place and get evidence that would close you down forever. Something they didn't do before because of André Gauvreau's connections, I suspect.

MADAM. You're a very intuitive man, Mr. Rick. But why do you want to find André's murderer? Not for the preservation of Café Noir.

RICK. I have my reasons. Were you and André a team?

MADAM. Once, yes. For a while I was his partner in life.

I was your typical radical college student, longing for a worthy cause to jump behind—to make sacrifices for. You know the standard fool-hearted romantic that colleges put out with as much volume as these islands grown bananas. Then I met André and his radical French political party. *(She begins running her hands through a male patron's hair, thinking only of André.)* He was a mature, handsome and sexy man, with piercing eyes and a hypnotic voice. The kind of man girls fall in love with easily. *(She finally notices the man is not André and looks disappointed. She walks away.)* He was everything I dreamed of and I gave him everything. I joined him and his fight for French liberté and found myself doing things I never thought I ever could or would do. Slowly politics gave way to smuggling. The black market was much more profitable than politics, and his political connections helped his enterprise flourish. Women have a weakness for dangerous men and he was mine. You can even surprise yourself at how far you'll go when you're hopelessly in love with someone. I never stopped loving him.

RICK. But he stopped loving you.

MADAM. Not stopped, just changed.

(GUTTERMAN enters.)

GUTTERMAN. Madam? It is imperative I speak to you. Someone has been in M. Gauvreau's office.

(MADAM looks very nervous. She quickly exits. GUTTERMAN glares at RICK and exits.)

RICK. *(To audience.)* The motives for André Gauvreau's murder were coming fast and furious. Unfortunately, the gal I had to clear was the last person seen with the deceased before he washed up on a beach with two slugs in him. But the violently jealous Thursby looked like a pill even the St. Vincent police would swallow. *(Suddenly two gunshots ring out.*

Through the front door staggers THURSBY—shot in the chest.) Although suddenly it looked like Thursby swallowed some lead. *(RICK runs to catch THURSBY.)* Who was it Thursby? Who?

(THURSBY leans against the radio.)

THURSBY. *(Dying.)* Too late—

RICK. Come on Thursby—cough it up—*(THURSBY coughs. RICK shakes his head disappointed.)* Spit it out—*(THURSBY spits. RICK looks even more annoyed.)* Sing—

(THURSBY turns on the radio. Tango music starts as THURSBY sings "IT WAS". He alternates from dying in RICK's arms to dancing with him. The rest of the cast enters to see what's happened.)

THURSBY. It was—it was—
THE CLICK OF THE BARREL
THE CRACK OF THE .22
YOU TURNED AT THE SOUND
AND FOUND IT WAS MEANT FOR YOU

I HAD A PLAN THAT COULD NOT FAIL
FINGER THE KILLER AND THEN TRY BLACKMAIL
BUT I WAS CARELESS AND THE KILLER DIDN'T CARE
I TOOK A HIT
NOW WAS THAT FAIR?

RICK. But who was it, Thursby?

THURSBY. It was—it was—

EVERYONE. *(Singing chorus in hushed tones.)*
THE CLICK OF THE BARREL
THE CRACK OF THE .22
YOU TURNED AT THE SOUND
AND FOUND IT WAS MEANT FOR YOU

THURSBY.
I SHOULDA SEEN IT COMING FROM THE START
YOU TRUST A KILLER
YOU GET SHOT IN THE HEART
BUT I KNOW WHO PLUGGED ME
I CAN PROVE IT AS WELL
OKAY, I DIE
BUT WHAT THE HELL
(Cough.)

RICK. *(Impatient.)* WHO WAS IT?
THURSBY. It was—it was—
EVERYONE.
THE CLICK OF THE BARREL
THE CRACK OF THE .22
YOU TURNED AT THE SOUND
AND FOUND IT WAS MEANT FOR YOU

THURSBY.
I WANTED TO TAKE MARIA FAR FROM THIS
HOW COULD I KNOW THE KILLER WOULDN'T MISS
HONESTLY. WHAT I DID
I DID FOR LOVE
BUT NOW I'M ICED
COURTESY OF ...
RICK. *(Irritated.)* Of who, Thursby? Who was it?
THURSBY. It was—it was—

(As the cast sings the chorus, THURSBY pulls a gray envelope(s) out of his coat and slips it to RICK. (If crowd decided for RICK to get CAIRO's envelope, THURSBY will give him only one. If the crowd decided for RICK not to go for the envelope, THURSBY will give him two gray envelopes.)

EVERYONE. *(All getting bored and impatient.)*
THE CLICK OF A BARREL
THE CRACK OF THE .22
YOU TURNED AT THE SOUND
AND FOUND IT WAS MEANT FOR YOU

RICK. Who was it?

THURSBY.
IT WAS
IT WAS
IT WAS—

(THURSBY rolls his eyes and drips dead.)

RICK. When I said sing, I didn't mean literally.

(RICK turns off the radio then closes THURSBY's eyes. MARIA runs up as RICK lowers THURSBY to the ground. RICK hides the envelope.)

MARIA. *(Crying.)* Thursby? THURSBY!

(MARIA falls over the body in tears. CAIRO walks to the body.)

CAIRO. Poor boy. I'm terribly sorry, Maria.

(CAIRO swipes THURSBY's wallet as he steps away.)

GUTTERMAN. It's what comes from living the way he did. Live by the sword, die by the sword and all that.

SHEILA. Shut up, Gutterman.

(MARIA stands up, holding THURSBY's gun. She points it at each of the characters, not sure who to shoot, who is responsible. As everyone steps back, RICK steps forward. He slowly takes the gun from her trembling hands. She cries in his shoulder.)

MARIA. Someone must pay for this, Mr. Rick. Promise me you'll find out who?

RICK. It's a promise, Maria.

(RICK motions for SHEILA, who takes MARIA off as she continues to cry.)

GUTTERMAN. One shouldn't make promises that one can't keep, Mr. Rick.

RICK. I never do, Mr. Gutterman. I never do.

MADAM. I think we should remove Mr. Thursby from the dining area. I'm sure the St. Vincent health officials would agree. Mr. Gutterman, Mr. Cairo?

(GUTTERMAN and CAIRO move forward and pick up THURSBY.)

MADAM. We'll leave him in André's office until the St. Vincent police get here.

(MADAM leads CAIRO and GUTTERMAN out, with the deceased THURSBY between them. RICK pulls out the two gray envelopes. HE opens one and out slides some black & white negatives and piece of ledger paper. He holds them up to the light and looks very interested. Just as RICK is about to open the other envelope, GUTTERMAN enters behind him.)

GUTTERMAN. Well, Mr. Rick! Perhaps it's time we had a chat.

(RICK pockets the envelopes again.)

RICK. About what, Mr. Gutterman?

GUTTERMAN. About the envelopes illegally obtained from André Gauvreau's office. As the Café Noir's legal counsel, I am executor of M. Gauvreau's estate. Therefore I must warn you that the removal or exposure of any—

RICK. Exposure? And what's in these alleged missing envelopes?

(MARIA has entered.)

MARIA. *(Revenge in her eyes.)* Memoirs André kept on some of his dear friends. *(MARIA pulls two gray envelopes from behind her back. She opens them and pulls out police records, which she starts passing out to a number of tables. GUTTERMAN looks horrified at her actions and begins trying to retrieve all the papers. CAIRO and SHEILA enter and start collecting the papers MARIA hands out as well.)* You'll never collect them all. He kept copies everywhere—insurance against any wise guy who might think they could steal away the hold he had on them. I'm sure there are more—possibly even hidden under each table. *(To Patron.)* Go on, look.

(There are envelopes taped under each table. Inside are police records on MARIA, SHEILA, MADAM, GUTTERMAN and CAIRO. RICK begins to look at one. Seeing the many envelopes, the characters give up trying to collect them. MARIA exits. Angry with her, SHEILA, CAIRO and GUTTERMAN follow.)

MADAM. It'll take some time before the St. Vincent police sails over here. We should take the opportunity to have the next course. With any luck, we may get out of having to serve dinner to the entire police force.

(MADAM claps. Lights out. Entree is served.
Just before the next scene begins, VANGILDER enters. He reads the police records on the tables. If questioned, he'll introduce himself as a Dutch businessman from St. Maarten.)

Scene 3

(Music intro. Lights up. RICK is reading a few of the reports. VANGILDER intercepts SHEILA on her way towards the kitchen.)

VANGILDER. Schickelmeier, Ja?
SHEILA. Excuse me.

(SHEILA tries to get around VANGILDER, but he blocks her.)

VANGILDER. Ja! Der eyes, dat nose. Mrs. Schickelmeier's missing daughter. Nancy.
SHEILA. My name is Sheila. Now if you'll excuse me.

(SHEILA gets past him, but his next line stops her in her tracks. RICK starts to move closer to listen.)

VANGILDER. Your name is Sheilda. Nancy is you mutter. I just left her in St. Maarten vere she's recovering. She's always recovering, your mutter.
SHEILA. What do you want?
VANGILDER. It's really a question of what you don't vant, isn't it? I read in der paper about die unfortunate death of Herr Gauvreau. He vas a business acquaintance.
SHEILA. Then you must be a criminal.
VANGILDER. It's criminal vhat an impetuous girl might do to her fatter's reputation. *(He holds up a police report on her.)* Surprising what business opportunities a spur of der moment trip might bring, Ja?
SHEILA. My name is Sheila Wonderly.

(VANGILDER laughs at her. RICK comes forward and grabs him by the lapels.)

RICK. Listen, slime face. If the lady says her name is Sheila Wonderly, it's Sheila Wonderly. *(Noticing the resemblance to THURSBY.)* You know, you sort of look like— *(VANGILDER quickly reaches into his coat, but RICK is faster and he reaches inside VANGILDER's coat and crushes his hand. Then RICK reaches in with his other hand and pulls out a small gun. RICK continues to crush VANGILDER's hand, causing him to wince.)* For me? How sweet. It's a little small, don't you think? But I bet everything about a guy like you is small.

(During the last lines MADAM entered.)

MADAM. Release him, Mr. Rick.

(RICK looks at her, then at VANGILDER. He releases VANGILDER, who rubs his hand just like THURSBY did.)

MADAM. You look a lot like—

VANGILDER. Madam Toureau, Ja?

MADAM. Ja—I mean yes. And you are?

VANGILDER. Herr Vangilder. Perhaps you've heard André speak of me?

(There is a look of recognition, and worry, on the MADAM's face.)

MADAM. Perhaps, Herr Vangilder.

VANGILDER. Zen perhaps ve could talk. In private.

MADAM. If you'll follow me.

(MADAM exits. VANGILDER goes after her, but stops and turns to RICK.)

VANGILDER. Mein gun, Mr. Rick?

RICK. Sorry. It's mine now. Something to remember you by.

(VANGILDER smiles menacingly at RICK and then at SHEILA. He laughs and exits after the MADAM.)

SHEILA. You know my names' not Wonderly, don't you?

RICK. Your father hired me to find you.

SHEILA. I hope he's paying you well. He can afford it.

RICK. So what makes a rich girl like you change into a—a—

SHEILA. Too polite to say it? What phrase do they use on TV now. Working girl? Pro? Streetwalker? My father is filthy rich, Ricky baby. And he got that way by promising people something no one could deliver—salvation. My father is a big time evangelist. Bet he didn't tell you that, did he?

RICK. Actually, no.

SHEILA. He raised me strict and narrow to be a proper little girl. Seen and never heard. My mother and I were part of his image, and image sells—just look at political elections. But we were just image—his business always came first and we were left alone, isolated from the rest of the sinful world. My mother became an alcoholic. My father became worried what effect she might have on me, so he sent me to college in Grenada to become a nurse. Suddenly I discovered a world I didn't know existed, the world I was sheltered from and therefore couldn't cope with. I became addicted to sex, got wasted on drugs and flunked out of college. I couldn't go back. Not to my pious father. So I went further into the hole he dug for me by protecting me too much. André got me out of a jam I got into after stowing away on board a luxury liner and making a mint on my back from wealthy retirees whose wives were busy shopping or playing shuffleboard. He even got me off the drugs. He looked out for me.

(RICK pulls an envelope out and displays the negatives.)

RICK. He also blackmailed your father with these photographs. There's even a record of when he sent your father the pictures and when payments were received. *(SHEILA looks at RICK, mad. She tries to grab the envelope, but RICK keeps it from her.)* And yet you loved André, along with a host of his friends from what I've heard. *(SHEILA tries to slap RICK, but he catches her hand.)* Sorry, sweetheart. Slapping is reserved for ladies.

(SHEILA pulls her hand away.)

SHEILA. No woman was a lady around André. He got more ass than a toilet seat at Grand Central Station. There's not a good looking dame in this part of the Caribbean that hasn't watched the sunrise from André's bed. *(To a woman patron.)* Isn't that right? Come on, don't play dumb with me, sister. You left with André two nights ago. And this doll over here, *(She goes to another female patron.)* She had all of last weekend with him. Needless to say, there are plenty of men that wanted André dead because of the plenty of women that found him alive.

RICK. But you left with him alive last night and this morning he washed up dead. That puts you in a tight spot.

SHEILA. I don't like you, Mr. Rick.

RICK. Sure you do. In fact, you love me. You just don't know it yet.

(SHEILA turns her back to him and smiles at the audience.)

SHEILA. Why, in God's name, would I ever love you?

RICK. Because I'm gonna get you out of this mess—the one André and his murder got you into.

(SHEILA leans back against RICK, flirting.)

SHEILA. Where's your shining armor? Or do you fancy yourself more the Bogart type, and I'm your femme fatale? *(Sensuously.)* Forget it. You're not my type.

RICK. And what, exactly, is your type?

(MARIA turns on the radio sings COLD AND STIFF—Making fun of SHEILA. As she sings, VANGILDER, MADAM, GUTTERMAN and CAIRO enter to watch her. She roams around and flirts with the audience.)

MARIA.
SHE LIKES 'EM COLD
SHE LIKES 'EM STIFF
SHE LIKES 'EM BETTER IF
THE GUYS AIN'T BREATHIN'
SO MANY OF HER MEN END UP THAT WAY
QUITE A COINCIDENCE
WOULDN'T YOU SAY
SHE LIKES 'EM STIFF
SHE LIKES 'EM COLD
A GUY DON'T GET TOO OLD
HE JUST GETS WASTED
SHE SEEMS TO RUN THROUGH THE FELLAS FAST
IT'S SUCH A SHAME THAT HER AFFAIRS DON'T LAST
ALL I CAN TELL YOU IS, BASED ON HER PAST
SHE LIKES 'EM COLD AND STIFF

SHE LIKES 'EM COLD
SHE LIKES 'EM STIFF
IT'S SO MUCH BETTER IF HE'S HORIZONTAL
SOME OTHER GIRL WILL WANT A MAN WHO TREATS HER NICE
HER, SHE SEEMS TO LIKE HER MEN AS COLD AS ICE
SHE LIKES 'EM HARD

AS HARD AS NAILS
SHE NEVER FAILS TO FIND
A GUY WHO BUYS IT
SHE CROOKS HER FINGER AND THE FOOLS COME 'ROUND
ITS NOT TOO LONG BEFORE THEY'RE ALL SHOT DOWN
IT ALWAYS HAPPENS WHEN SHE'S OUT OF TOWN
WATCH OUT, MY FRIEND
IT CAN HAPPEN AGAIN
SHE LIKES 'EM COLD AND STIFF AND DEAD!

(When the song ends MARIA is standing near VANGILDER [the others are all close behind or beside him]. The lights go out and everyone applauds. When the lights come up, VANGILDER has a strange stare on his face.)

GUTTERMAN. I always liked the way you sing, Maria.

MARIA. Why, thank you, Gutterman. I believe that's the first nice thing you've ever said to me.

(Suddenly, VANGILDER falls forward. A butcher's knife is sticking out of his back. RICK dashes forward and catches VANGILDER.)

RICK. Hang in there, Vangilder. Why did you come here? Who were you trying to put the touch on?

VANGILDER. It was—it was—

CAIRO. If he sings I'll shoot him. *(Everyone stares at CAIRO.)* I just don't like dying songs. They're so depressing.

(VANGILDER dies. But he presses something into RICK's hand as he goes.)

GUTTERMAN. Well, Madam Toureau. It looks like André's office will have matching bookends.

(GUTTERMAN and CAIRO bend down and pick up VANGILDER.)

CAIRO. Doesn't he sort of look like—
GUTTERMAN. Not in the least.

(CAIRO and GUTTERMAN exit, dragging VANGILDER between them.)

SHEILA. Do people always die when they meet you, Mr. Rick?

RICK. Only when they have important information that I haven't gotten yet. So play it safe and don't keep any secrets from me.

*(**VERSION A**—To go for the envelope: Continues with this scene)*
*(**VERSION B**—To tail SHEILA: Skip to stage direction, bottom of next page.)*

RICK. Actually, I'm not surprised to find you in a place like this.

SHEILA. Where would you be surprised to find me?

RICK. A convent for one, but certainly not in a dead man's café.

SHEILA. Some men, even when they're dead, can control a woman.

RICK. And you like it that way.

SHEILA. Why would I?

RICK. Because then you can blame whatever trouble you're in on someone else, someone who isn't around to say otherwise.

SHEILA. *(Leaning in, her lips almost touching his.)* You're such a smart guy, aren't you, Mr. Rick? Always knowing what to say—how to say it—who to say it to. What do you want, a medal?

RICK. I can think of something I'd like a whole lot more. Something a lot softer—wetter—sweeter.

(SHEILA licks RICK's lips.)

SHEILA. Something like that?

RICK. Something like that. And something like this.

(RICK kisses SHEILA. She bites his lip. He yells and steps back.)

RICK. But not that.

SHEILA. I thought you were a tough guy.

(SHEILA starts to leave.)

RICK. You think all guys are tough guys, so you can be heartless towards them before they can be heartless towards you.

SHEILA. What do you know?

RICK. I know you're running away but never getting anywhere. Because what you're really running away from is always right behind you, like your shadow, only deeper.

SHEILA. Don't pretend to know me, Mr. Just Plain Rick.

(SHEILA turns to leave again.)

RICK. I never pretend.

(SHEILA exits. RICK rubs his lip.)

*(**BOTH VERSIONS** continue here.)*

(GUTTERMAN enters.)

GUTTERMAN. Madam. The police have arrived at the back entrance. They've requested an interview with each of us. I advise we make a minimal compliance to avoid potentially further and more damaging investigation by the authorities.

MADAM. What ever you advise, Mr. Gutterman.

(MADAM, SHEILA and MARIA all exit. RICK starts to go as well, but GUTTERMAN stops him.)

GUTTERMAN. Mr. Rick? What a peculiar name.

RICK. It's Archer. Richard Archer, but everyone seems to call me Rick.

GUTTERMAN. Not everyone, Mr. Archer. Perhaps now we can have that chat?

RICK. I suppose it would be preferable to chatting with the St. Vincent police. Tell me, Gutterman, how do you fit in here? What did André have on you?

(During GUTTERMAN's next speech, he roams about the audience.)

GUTTERMAN. *(Short laugh.)* Nothing, Mr. Archer. Nothing at all. If you must know, I found myself here by accident. I was a successful barrister in the courts of London, managing some of the most prestigious trusts and estates of the most established families in Britain. Yes—I may not have had the glamor of your Perry Mason, but I assure you, I was financially much better off. To this I brought one unfortunate weakness—the love of ladies. Not those self-centered young and beautiful bimbos that present society admires with awe and envy. No, no Mr. Archer. I love that rare commodity of a true lady—

(GUTTERMAN stops at a mature older woman, whose hand he takes and kisses.)

GUTTERMAN. *(Cont.)* Who has had time to learn about the real world—who understands that there is a difference between desire and accessibility. The world has long since stopped producing this type of woman, Mr. Archer. So when I find one, I find myself doing anything for them—anything. *(To woman.)* Tonight, your place, midnight. Wear some pearls. *(Back to RICK.)* But as I was saying. Unfortunately, the well established families of Britain possessed just a few too many such women and my indiscretions lead to social humiliation and a significant loss of clientele. I decided I needed to go far away, someplace where I could start anew. Barbados was about as far as what little savings I had left would afford me. It was there I met Madam Toureau and soon found myself representing this establishment. But enough of me, Mr. Archer, it's time for us to discuss what *we* have to discuss.

RICK. Pardon my ignorance, but what is that?

GUTTERMAN. That is this.

(GUTTERMAN pulls a gun and points it at RICK, who raises his hands.)

GUTTERMAN. As they say each year in Hollywood—the envelope, please.

(RICK reaches into his pocket and pulls out VANGILDER's gun, pointing it at GUTTERMAN—who looks confused.)

RICK. You must be new at this, Gutterman. Never let your pigeon reach into his own pocket until you've patted him down. He might pull out a gun too, and then where are you?

(GUTTERMAN looks nervous and moves slowly. RICK stays opposite him—both guns always trained on each other, with a table of patrons between them.)

GUTTERMAN. And where are we then, Mr. Archer?

RICK. Between a rock and a hard place, otherwise called a stalemate.

(GUTTERMAN pulls a hanky out of his pocket and mops his brow. His hand slips a little, but tightens up quickly. Aiming the guns at each other, they begin to turn slowly, like circling birds of prey.)

GUTTERMAN. I warn you, Mr. Archer. At this range it would be terribly unlikely for me to miss. I must insist that you give me the envelope.

RICK. For either of us to miss. What's so important about the envelope? Everyone here already knows the contents of the envelope, Maria made sure of that.

GUTTERMAN. The police records? *(A short laugh.)* If it is already public record, of what possible importance could it be? The other gray envelope, Mr. Archer.

RICK. The one with the pictures of Sheila? Are you going to start dealing in pornography, Gutterman?

GUTTERMAN. *(Growing more impatient.)* Obviously not that gray envelope, Mr. Archer!

RICK. Well we're running out of gray envelopes. Perhaps you should send someone over to a stationery store. Maybe get something a little more colorful.

GUTTERMAN. *(Now angry.)* This is not a joking matter, Mr. Archer. I assure you, I am deadly serious.

RICK. And three people are seriously dead.

GUTTERMAN. In a moment it may be four. *(GUTTERMAN raises his gun and aims between RICK's eyes. RICK raises his gun to between GUTTERMAN's eyes. Gutterman continues, scared.)* Five? The choice is yours.

(GUTTERMAN cocks his gun. RICK looks nervous—then turns to the audience. GUTTERMAN freezes.)

RICK. Okay, folks. Here we go again. By a show of hands, how many think I should hand over the envelope to our ambiguous attorney here? *(There will be a show of hands.)* And how many say I call this buffoon's bluff?

(There will be a show of hands. RICK turns back to GUTTERMAN, who becomes alive again. GUTTERMAN mops his brow again. RICK reaches into his pocket and pulls out the envelope. He pauses, then RICK touches the edge of the envelope in the flame of a candle on a nearby table. As it burns, RICK drops it into a wine ice bucket beside the table.)

RICK. *(Cont.)* If I can't see what's inside, no one can. Just call me a poor sport.

(GUTTERMAN looks at the burning envelope, then begins to laugh.)

GUTTERMAN. Very good, Mr. Archer. Yes, yes—very good indeed.

(RIGFIELD enters [the same actor as THURSBY but disguised] dressed in a trench coat. He flashes a badge at the audience. Speaks with a British accent.)

RIGFIELD. Police! Deputy Inspector Rigfield, Kingstown dispatch.

(GUTTERMAN and RICK quickly hide their guns before RIGFIELD notices them. GUTTERMAN and RICK recognize the resemblance.)

RICK & GUTTERMAN. Doesn't he look like—?

(RIGFIELD looks about at the audience in disgust.)

RIGFIELD. This is the legendary Café Noir? They're right, it does cater to the lowest of the low. I have a few questions for you blokes, not that I'd trust any of your bloody answers.

(MADAM enters, annoyed. Followed by everyone else.)

MADAM. Deputy Inspector! We have an arrangement. No police, past the back office or the kitchen. We guarantee our patron's privacy.

RIGFIELD. Right! And I'd guarantee there's a lot of arrest warrants I could serve here.

MADAM. Dinner is the only thing being served here, Deputy Inspector. And your presence is spoiling everyone's appetite.

(Blackout.)

Scene 4

(Music intro. Lights up. Everyone is present.)

MADAM. Now, Deputy Inspector—no discussion, out you go.

RIGFIELD. But there's a small matter of two corpses in the back office that I'd say warrants some discussion.

SHEILA. Do you have a discussion warrant, *Deputy* Inspector?

RIGFIELD. Don't be frivolous with the law, young lady.

GUTTERMAN. But perhaps Ms. Wonderly has a point. After all, you do need a search warrant to search and—

CAIRO. —and an arrest warrant to make an arrest. Why not a discussion warrant to warrant a discussion?

MARIA. Sounds logical to me. Where's your discussion warrant, *Deputy* Inspector?

RIGFIELD. You're all bloody balmy! Now, look here, I'm the assigned constable and I demand some cooperation.

MADAM. Mr. Gutterman is our attorney and legal counsel, *Deputy* Inspector.

GUTTERMAN. And as such, *Deputy* Inspector Rigfield, I have already advised my clients to agree to make statements and to submit to some brief questioning. However, if you intend to use coercion and begin criminal interrogations, I must demand that either formal charges be lodged, through the proper channels, or I shall be forced to file charges of harassment and police intimidation, not to mention seeking damages for the projected loss of business revenues caused by your—

RIGFIELD. *(Infuriated.)* I just want to ask a few blasted questions! And what's the meaning of all this here emphasis everyone's placing on Deputy?

RICK. They're just getting your goat, Rigfield. And you're letting them.

RIGFIELD. And who the bloody hell do you think you are?

(RICK pulls out his license from his wallet and hands it to RIGFIELD.)

RICK. Richard Archer, private investigator. I was granted a temporary territorial extension by the St. Vincent authorities. You can check with the records division in Kingstown.

(RIGFIELD glances at license, then throws it back at RICK.)

RIGFIELD. I don't like balmy private licenses.

RICK. You sure like words beginning in B—blasted, balmy, bloody—

RIGFIELD. This is police business—

GUTTERMAN. Not until there are officially filed charges. At the moment, *Deputy* Inspector, you are merely responding to my call reporting the discovery of two corpses.

RIGFIELD. Discovery! They were both bloody iced right under your very noses, weren't they?

RICK. Listen, Rigfield. I've been working this place all night. I know how to deal with these characters and I think I can work it so that we both get what we came here for.

RIGFIELD. You can work it? Typical yank peeper, aren't you—coming in here telling us how to do our job?

SHEILA. Well, somebody better—you're making a real mess of it.

RIGFIELD. Look here! I'm not leaving until I find the person responsible for the death of those two stiffs holding up both ends of the bookcase in that back office.

RICK. How would you like to get André Gauvreau's murderer in the process? Maybe you wouldn't be stuck with that deputy prefix anymore.

RIGFIELD. You know who plugged Gauvreau?

RICK. I've got a damn good idea. If you give me fifteen minutes I'll hand you the whole thing in one nice neat package.

RIGFIELD. Right! Dream on, peeper.

(RICK pulls a gray envelope from his coat. RICK opens it and pulls out a deed.)

RICK. The deed to Café Noir is a buried treasure, Rigfield. It's not only the deed to this café but to a few square miles of land on Tobago Cay where André's body was found and where Resorts International is putting up a casino. *(To audience.)* I read it during the entree. *(To GUTTERMAN.)* I bet he stood to make a bundle off that sale.

GUTTERMAN. *(Short laugh.)* Mr. Archer, you're as bad as a good lawyer. He wanted to sell, but I convinced him to lease the land for a percentage take of the gross receipts. A very lucrative arrangement, one could even afford to go straight. I suppose the envelope you ignited merely contained a few embarrassing photographic negatives.

(SHEILA looks quickly at RICK, who returns her stare with a shrug.)

RICK. *(To SHEILA.)* I don't want pictures, I want the real thing.

SHEILA. The way you're playing your cards this evening you may just get it.

CAIRO. I'm disappointed in you, Mr. Rick. After I paid you to obtain that envelope—

RICK. Thursby got to it first, he handed it to me as he lost his final breath. He thought it would be his ticket out of here, which in a way it was. Unfortunately, it wasn't the way Thursby had hoped.

RIGFIELD. So Thursby was washed out for the dirty deed, eh?

RICK. Maybe, maybe not.

RIGFIELD. I thought you just spouted it's a virtual gold mine?

RICK. Sure it is. But as he was dying, Thursby also mentioned that he had figured who André's killer was.

RIGFIELD. Dead men tell no tales eh?

MADAM. Such a way with words, Deputy Inspector.

RICK. André was shot twice, right, Rigfield?

RIGFIELD. And how, wise guy, did you know that?

RICK. It was in the paper. I'd guess André's killer was someone he was well acquainted with.

RIGFIELD. Fair enough guess. The bullets entered from a lower angle, some powder even discovered on the outside of his suit jacket. The talking end of that barrel was bloody close. His wallet was still on him, quite a bit of cash in it too, along with his watch and most of his jewelry.

RICK. What calibre? *(RICK pulls out VANGILDER's gun and hands it to RIGFIELD, who looks at RICK, shocked.)* Vangilder's piece—it's a .32, never fired. Mr. Gutterman's gun, on the other hand—

(GUTTERMAN pulls his gun and points it at RICK. Then he gives his short laugh and hands it to RIGFIELD.)

GUTTERMAN. A .38—and it's not even loaded.

RIGFIELD. Doesn't mean you couldn't have used a different rod to plug André and then Thursby. The ventilation in Thursby looks like the .22 variety.

RICK. Vangilder knew André and that he had a few secrets over some of his friends. Hearing of André's death, Vangilder thought he could use that information to make a quick killing—which is exactly what somebody here did to him—cutting him out of the picture with a butchers knife borrowed from the kitchen. Who knows what, if anything, Vangilder really knew. But after Thursby, panic started setting in on our killer, who decided not to take any chances.

RIGFIELD. Think you're real smart, eh peeper? Vangilder didn't *hear* about Gauvreau's death. He was the bloke that found the body. Vangilder ran sightseeing boat tours—as well as a little smuggling on the side.

RICK. *(Remembering something.)* You said most of André's jewelry was on him. What was missing?

RIGFIELD. Well, nothing for sure. But there was a band of white about his suntanned left ring finger.

GUTTERMAN. Isn't it true, Maria, that a personal effect of the victim is utilized in the employment of a voodoo doll?

CAIRO. What are you implying, Mr. Gutterman?

(MARIA gives GUTTERMAN a deadly stare. GUTTERMAN gives his short laugh.)

GUTTERMAN. Perhaps, Deputy Inspector, you should be made aware of Maria's talents and the source of her major income—the ancient art of voodoo.

MARIA. It is a religion.

MADAM. Is that what you were doing at closing last night when you snapped that chicken's neck in the kitchen? You can sell anything you want here, Maria, but no practicing of rituals. We've been through all this before.

SHEILA. *(Realization.)* You're the one who threw the chicken blood on André and me from the shadows last night! You witch, you ruined my favorite dress.

(SHEILA starts for MARIA. RICK stops her.)

MARIA. I'll ruin more than that if you killed my Thursby.
SHEILA. Oh, right—what, with your evil eye?
CAIRO. Do not jest! Ms. LaRue is quite famous in these parts. Her magic has never failed.
MARIA. As it did not fail you last night, Mr. Cairo.
RIGFIELD. What does she mean by that?
CAIRO. I assure you, Inspector, it's nothing—nothing at all.
RIGFIELD. It's definitely something, if you've started calling me Inspector.
MARIA. André Gauvreau died last night, did he not?
RIGFIELD. He was murdered last night.
MARIA. But he is dead—thus the spell took and the money is mine.
RIGFIELD. Spell? Money?
GUTTERMAN. Our Maria only collects if her spells work, Deputy Inspector.
RICK. How much did you pay her, Cairo? What's the going rate for a voodoo doll?
CAIRO. I don't have a voodoo doll. You can search me if you like.
GUTTERMAN. But when I arrived at the beginning of this evening, I saw Mr. Cairo with a small wrapped bundle.
RICK. And what was in that bundle? Anyone see a small wrapped bundle lying about this place?

(The table where the doll was left will be asked by RIGFIELD, as if by random. The table will reveal the bundle. If they haven't opened it, RIGFIELD will. If they have opened it, RIGFIELD will take it.)

MADAM. *(Perplexed.)* Two pins, in the chest—exactly where André was shot! *(MADAM stares at MARIA.)* But how could—

(Pause.)

RIGFIELD. She could have made the doll after the report of the murder.

SHEILA. *(Perplexed.)* No—I saw her putting the pins in that doll last night, after closing—just before I left with André. I didn't really think too much about it at the time. Maria was always doing strange things.

RIGFIELD. Like not only putting two pins in the doll, but two slugs in the deceased as well?

GUTTERMAN. Let us not forget that it was Mr. Cairo who wanted M. Gauvreau dead enough to pay for her magical touch.

CAIRO. Everyone here wanted Gauvreau dead! Why is everyone picking on me?

RICK. Not everyone. It's Gutterman who's focusing all the attention on you, Cairo. Like a fox trying to throw off the hounds.

GUTTERMAN. *(Short laugh.)* You amuse me, Mr. Archer. Of course I had a motive, but so did everyone else here, including your Ms. Wonder-lay.

RICK. But the question is who had enough motive to bump off Thursby and Vangilder as well. And of what importance is the thing Vangilder slipped me as his life slipped from him?

(RICK pulls out an earring—that matches the one MADAM returned to SHEILA in Scene 1. SHEILA is about to claim it, but stops herself. She gives RICK a guilty look as he hands the earring to RIGFIELD, whose attention is solely on the earring.)

RIGFIELD. It's the balmy earring we found on the beach

by the corpse. We thought it got washed away with the tide while we were fending off those bloody albatrosses. Vangilder must have pinched it. This case has me stymied. A two bit thug that gets wasted by the same gun that washed away Gauvreau, five suspects who'd raise a glass to his demise rather than attend his wake, a voodoo doll with two pins right where the deceased took two slugs to the chest and a disappearing earring that turns up on a dead blackmailer.

(SHEILA turns to look at the MADAM, as if to say "please don't tell." The MADAM refuses to look at SHEILA.)

MADAM. Well, Deputy Inspector Rigfield. With you on the case, I'm sure everyone will get their just desserts.

(The lights fade so only RICK is lit again in his spotlight. The others all freeze in place.)

RICK. Their just desserts? Isn't that what criminal investigation is all about? It's certainly one of the reasons murder mysteries are so popular. In a world full of confusion and corruption, only the mystery guarantees that in the end everything will become clear and good will triumph over evil. That's what made me want to become a detective in the first place. But in real life nothing is clear and all too often evil reaps the rewards while the good suffer the injustices. I knew whose earring that was, alright. And it was only a matter of time before Rigfield and the rest of the St. Vincent police put the picture together for themselves. But what was the real picture? André Gauvreau was a rotten man who left behind five lost people with some solid motives to deep six him. But only one of them had pulled the trigger of a small .22 that sent André on an eternal vacation to Hades. My question to you is, which one?

(Blackout. If dinner is offered dessert is served. Whether or not dessert is served, lights come up and characters move about the audience, implicating each other. RICK and RIGFIELD will go around and collect all the "whodunit and why" guesses.)

GUTTERMAN implicates Sheila—the blackmail photos

CAIRO implicates Gutterman—that André cut Gutterman out of the casino deal.

MADAM implicates CAIRO—he knew his true identity.

MARIA implicates MADAM—the woman scorned.

SHEILA implicates MARIA—André blew up the police station and pinned the crime on Maria's mother, who died in prison.

RICK asks patrons who they think did it.

Scene 5
The Finale

(After all guesses have been collected, a short musical intro will signal the beginning of the last scene. All characters will resume the same position they had at the end of the last scene. RIGFIELD addresses the audience.)

RIGFIELD. Does anyone recognize this earring or remember who it might belong to?

(Hopefully someone will say it belongs to SHEILA. It is possible someone will be confused and say it belonged to MADAM or MARIA. RIGFIELD will show the earring to whoever the audience points out and ask if it's theirs. If SHEILA, she'll say it looks a little like one she lost. If MADAM,

she'll say she returned one just like it to SHEILA—who lost it last night. If MARIA, she'll say it looks like the kind SHEILA wears. If the audience doesn't know, the scene will just continue with GUTTERMAN.)

GUTTERMAN. *(Short laugh.)* I remember thinking how lovely you looked in them last night, Ms. Wonderly.

SHEILA. Thanks a lot, Gutterman. Tell me, what's my motive? I seem to have forgotten.

GUTTERMAN. The pictures André used to blackmail your righteous father, of course, Kid!

CAIRO. But you—you wanted a part of that casino deal.

GUTTERMAN. I set up that deal! André would have squandered the whole thing!

CAIRO. But all André was giving you was nothing more than your simple retainer.

MADAM. And you, Mr. Cairo, tried everything to break André's hold over you—the knowledge of your true identity. Something that was never tangible, but locked inside André's head.

MARIA. And you, Madam, are the woman scorned—the unrequited love of the wife André rejected to chase after cheap peaches like Ms. Wonderly, which he devoured before your very eyes night after night.

SHEILA. And you, Maria, hated André because it was him and his Liberté party that bombed a police station years ago—an event that resulted in your mother's death. Any one of you could have picked up my lost earring last night and planted it on the beach next to André's corpse.

RIGFIELD. And you could have lost it there yourself.

RICK. Come on, Rigfield. You're a smart guy. I know you've figured who the murderer is.

RIGFIELD. I have?

RICK. Sure, I can follow your thinking. I don't know either if it was coincidence or something more arcane that explained the pins in Maria's doll being so accurate. But I do know that neither the newspaper, nor you, Rigfield, ever mentioned exactly where André was shot. All that was ever said was two bullet wounds, which could have been in the back, head, neck, side—. But when Maria's doll was revealed, our killer slipped up by remarking out loud that the pins were in the chest, exactly how André was shot. Yeah, you're a sharp guy to catch that Rigfield—because then all the other pieces fell into place. Like the person who's the last person to have left this place last night would be the most likely one to pick up a pair of lost earrings. And only that one person would stand to gain both financially and emotionally by pumping two .22 slugs into André's chest and then bother to slip a ring off his left ring finger—his wedding ring, no doubt. You can even surprise yourself at how far you'll go when you're hopelessly in love with someone—that's what you told me earlier this evening, Madam Toureau. I guess you went pretty damn far last night, didn't you?

(MADAM smiles sadly.)

MADAM. I'm sure you'll make full inspector in no time, Deputy Inspector Rigfield.

(MADAM pulls a small gun out and points it at RIGFIELD.)

MADAM. But I'm not really cut out for prison, even on St. Vincent Island. I'm sorry, Maria—I didn't know you loved Thursby that much. Maybe if I had I wouldn't have panicked. You're a smart guy, Mr. Rick. *(She turns the gun on him.)* Do me a favor?

(SHEILA hides behind RICK.)

RICK. Sure. It's hard to refuse a lady with a loaded gun.

MADAM. Make sure Café Noir stays open. There really is a place for it in a world as messed up as this one.

(MADAM turns the gun into her chest and fires it. GUTTERMAN dashes to catch her and lowers her down.)

GUTTERMAN. *(Broken hearted.)* Madam? Oh, my beloved lady! Why? I could have gotten you off with a plea bargain. I could have—tried.

MADAM. *(Dying.)* It was—it is—too late.

(The lights fade out and the spotlight comes back up on RICK.)

RICK. I never collected the rest of the money from Sheila's father. Because when I make someone a promise—as unusual as this may sound in this day and age—I keep it. I never promised the Reverend I'd bring back his little girl, just find her—which I did. But I made someone else a promise that night. A promise to a woman with her own philosophy on life and her own code of ethics. A promise I've kept to this day. *(He starts to slip on a white dinner jacket.)* So if ever you get down to the lesser known islands of the eastern Caribbean, stop by Mustique in the Grenadines *(SHEILA steps forward with a pair of drinks, handing one to RICK.)* and my co-manager Sheila and I will give you a drink on the house—at the Café Noir.

(RICK and SHEILA toast and kiss as the music comes up and the lights fade out. Lights up, cast bow, announcement of the winning sleuth and awarding of prize.)

END OF PLAY

PROPERTY LIST

NOTE: All props should be as realistic as possible, but in color black, white or a shade of gray or silver, if possible. The switch blade and the three guns should all be metal and menacing looking, otherwise the tension of each scene will be lost.

SCENE 1

Newspaper excerpt—one for every table
Envelope—stuffed
Bundle with voodoo doll inside
Cigarette and match
Earring
Switch blade—Thursby's
Foreign looking money
Key on gray ribbon
Airline size bottle of vodka
Small jar of caviar
Electronic appliance catalogue
Gun or weapons catalogue
Voodoo charms—small figures, strange beads, etc.

SCENE 2

Glass of water
Gray envelope with B&W negatives and ledger page inside
Gray envelope
Gray envelope with police records inside (one for Maria, and one under every table)

SCENE 3

Small gun—Vangilder's
Butcher's knife—rigged in Vangilder's back
Small gun—Gutterman's
Candle (to burn envelope in)
Police badge

SCENE 4
P.I. License
Gray envelope with deed inside
Earring—matching scene 1

SCENE 5 - Finale
Small gun—Madam's (working .22 starters pistol)

CAFÉ NOIR HOLIDAY JOKES

SCENE 1
RICK: And that's how I ended up spending Christmas eve here, at the Café Noir.

SHEILA: I was detained!
MADAM: By a fat guy in a red suit and 12 reindeer?

RICK. To earn the rest of my clams I had to get close to her and get her out of the mess she was in deeper than she knew. What a way to spend the holidays!

MADAM: And what makes you think I could use a stranger in my place?
RICK: The holiday rush, and I read—

MADAM: She carved up her stepparents on the night before Christmas and served them to their relatives the next day.

THURSBY: Who are you?
SHEILA: Something Maria wants to slip into her stockings a little early. *(To RICK.)* Oh, this is Thursby—

RICK: Breaking into a dead man's office doesn't seem like that small a gesture to me?
CAIRO: Where's your holiday spirit? And what if an elf were to give you the key?

SCENE 2.

MADAM: *(After THURSBY dies.)* Put him by the fireplace in the back office.

SCENE 3

RICK: *(Taking gun from VANGILDER.)* A present for me? How sweet. But it's a little small don't you think?

SHEILA. And this doll, she spent last weekend wrapping his holiday presents, while he was unwrapping hers.

GUTTERMAN: *(Removing VANGILDER.)* Well, it looks like André's fireplace will have matching fire irons.

RICK: Well we're running out of gray envelopes. Why don't you send someone down to the stationery store and get some with a holiday motif?

RICK: *(Taking out envelope to hand to GUTTERMAN, after vote.)* Merry Christmas. *(He burns the envelope.)*
RICK: Oops, how clumsy of me. I'm afraid I can't get you another one because I didn't wrap it. Maybe I can get you a gift certificate from Blackmailers-r-us?

RICK: I don't want photos. I want the whole package.
SHEILA. The way you're playing Santa Claus tonight, you may just get it, milk and cookies and all.

Other Publications for Your Interest

THE WHITE HOUSE MURDER CASE

(LITTLE THEATRE—MORALITY)

By JULES FEIFFER

9 men, 1 woman—Interior, interior inset.

The incisive satire of Jules Feiffer is here aimed at the war posture of the United States in some future time. The war this year is in Brazil, and the American poison gas attack backfires. The President is worried about what to tell the people on the eve of an election, how to explain the gas being in the "U.S. peace arsenal." A staunch old general, blinded and crippled by war, comes in and demonstrates by his stoicism the idiocy of outmoded codes. While the cabinet is concocting a cock-and-bull story for the people, the President's wife is murdered. The duplicity of the President then comes to the fore: "The crime must be solved and then an explanation for the United States people readied." In lieu of film strips of the war, there are life-size scenes, showing a C.I.A. man rescuing a foot soldier, and then the two of them getting to know one another—before they kill each other. "A very funny, very savage man. He takes a man-sized swipe at our modern society. There is so much that is brilliant in the conception of The White House Murder Case."—N.Y. Times. "Tremendously funny. A witty, wonderful comedy."—WCBS-TV.

ROMANTIC COMEDY

(LITTLE THEATRE—COMEDY)

By BERNARD SLADE

2 men, 4 women—Interior

Arrogant, self-centered and sharp-tongued Jason Carmichael, successful coauthor of Broadway romantic comedies is facing two momentous events; he's about to marry a society belle and his collaborator is retiring from the fray. Enter Phoebe Craddock, mousy Vermont schoolteacher and budding playwright, Presto! Jason acquires a talented and adoring collaborator. Fame and success are theirs for ten years and then Jason's world falls apart. His wife divorces him to go into politics (says Jason, "I married Grace Kelly and wound up with Bella Abzug")—and Phoebe, her love for Jason unrequited, marries a breezy journalist and moves to Paris. Jason goes into professional, financial and physical decline. Reenter a now chic and successful-in-her-own-right Phoebe—and guess the ending! Meaty roles for the supporting cast. Starred Tony Perkins and Mia Farrow on Broadway. "A darling of a play . . . zesty entertainment of cool wit and warm sentiment."—N.Y. Post. "An utterly disarming, lighthearted confection about love, friendship and theatrical trauma."—WWD. "It's brilliant comedy. It's also a hit. Funniest comedy on Broadway in years."—WABC-TV7. "Marvelously entertaining . . . very funny and touching."—WCBS-TV2.

New Comedies from Samuel French, Inc.

THE LADY IN QUESTION (Little Theatre.-Comedy)
by Charles Busch.
5m., 4f. 1 int., 1 ext. w/insert.

This hilarious spoof of every trashy damsel-in-distress-vs.-the Nazis movie you ever saw packed them in Off Broadway, where the irrepressible Mr. Busch starred as Gertrude Garnet, world-renowned concert pianist and world-class hedonist. On tour in Bavaria, Gertrude finds her Nazi hosts charming; until, that is, she unwittingly becomes enlisted in a plot by Prof Erik Maxwell to free his mother, a famous actress who has appeared in an anti-Nazi play, from the clutches of the Fuhrer's fearsome minions. At first, Gertrude is more concerned about the whereabouts of her missing cosmetics bag; but when her best friend and travelling companion Kitty is murdered by the Nazi swine, Gertrude agrees to help Erik by manipulating the Nazi Baron Von Elsner, whose mansion becomes the escape route. Of course, Gertrude and Erik fall in love; and, of course, there is a desperate dash (on *skis*, no less!) to the safety of the Swiss border, where Gertrude and Erik find True Love. Mr. Busch's send-up of this film genre is so witty and well-constructed that, as the NY Times pointed out, it would be just as entertaining if the role of Gertrude were played by a woman. "Bewitchingly entertaining. I couldn't have had a better time, unless perhaps someone had given me popcorn."—N.Y. Post. "Hilarious."—N.Y. Times.
(#14182)

RED SCARE ON SUNSET (Advanced Groups-Comedy)
by Charles Busch.
5m., 3f. Unit set.

This Off-Broadway hit is set in 1950's Hollywood during the blacklist days. This is a hilarious comedy that touches on serious subjects by the author of *Vampire Lesbians of Sodom*. Mary Dale is a musical comedy star who discovers to her horror that her husband, her best friend, her director and houseboy are all mixed up in a communist plot to take over the movie industry. Among their goals is the dissolution of the star system! Mary's conversion from Rodeo Drive robot to McCarthy marauder who ultimately names names including her husband's makes for outrageous, thought provoking comedy. The climax is a wild dream sequence where Mary imagines she's Lady Godiva, the role in the musical she's currently filming. Both right and left are skewered in this comic melodrama. "You have to champion the ingenuity of Busch's writing which twirls twist upon twist and spins into comedy heaven."—Newsday.
(#19982)

Other Publications for Your Interest

NOISES OFF

(LITTLE THEATRE—FARCE)

By MICHAEL FRAYN

5 men, 4 women—2 Interiors

This wonderful Broadway smash hit is "a farce about farce, taking the clichés of the genre and shaking them inventively through a series of kaleidoscopic patterns. Never missing a trick, it has as its first act a pastiche of traditional farce; as its second, a contemporary variant on the formula; as its third, an elaborate undermining of it. The play opens with a touring company dress-rehearsing 'Nothing On', a conventional farce. Mixing mockery and homage, Frayn heaps into this play-within-a-play a hilarious melee of stock characters and situations. Caricatures—cheery char, outraged wife and squeaky blonde—stampede in and out of doors. Voices rise and trousers fall . . . a farce that makes you think as well as laugh."—London Times Literary Supplement. ". . . as side-splitting a farce as I have seen. Ever? *Ever.*"—John Simon, NY Magazine. "The term 'hilarious' must have been coined in the expectation that something on the order of this farce-within-a-farce would eventually come along to justify it."—N.Y. Daily News. "Pure fun."—N.Y. Post. "A joyous and loving reminder that the theatre really does go on, even when the show falls apart."—N.Y. Times. (#16052)

THE REAL THING

(ADVANCED GROUPS—COMEDY)

By TOM STOPPARD

4 men, 3 women—Various settings

The effervescent Mr. Stoppard has never been more intellectually—and *emotionally*—engaging than in this "backstage" comedy about a famous playwright named Henry Boot whose second wife, played on Broadway to great acclaim by Glenn Close (who won the Tony Award), is trying to merge "worthy causes" (generally a euphemism for left-wing politics) with her art as an actress. She has met a "political prisoner" named Brodie who has been jailed for radical thuggery, and who has written an inept play about how property is theft, about how the State stifles the Rights of The Individual, etc., etc., etc. Henry's wife wants him to make the play work theatrically, which he does after much soul-searching. Eventually, though, he is able to convince his wife that Brodie is emphatically *not* a victim of political repression. He is, in fact, a *thug*. Famed British actor Jeremy Irons triumphed in the Broadway production (Tony Award), which was directed to perfection by none other than Mike Nichols (Tony Award). "So densely and entertainingly packed with wit, ideas and feelings that one visit just won't do . . . Tom Stoppard's most moving play and the most bracing play anyone has written about love and marriage in years."—N.Y. Times. "Shimmering, dazzling theatre, a play of uncommon wit and intelligence which not only thoroughly delights but challenges and illuminates our lives."—WCBS-TV. 1984 Tony Award-Best Play. (#941)